Moholle Wala Ishq

Flairs and Glairs
Publication House

"Moholle Wala Ishq"

ISBN No: " 978-93-90416-98-1"
1ˢᵗ Edition
Language – English and Hindi

Flairs and Glairs
Publication House
Regd. Under MSME Act.

Disclaimer

This is a work of fiction and solely represent the thoughts of the corresponding authors of the articles.
Our editors have tried their best to edit the content of all the authors and check the plagiarism.
All the write-ups in this book are unique and are only published in this book.
In case any plagiarism or error is found, only the author is responsible alone, and not the publisher or the Compilers.

Cover Designing
Shubham Shah

Acknowledgement

Dear Almighty, thank you for blessing me with the power and zeal to be able to complete this Anthology. Also, Thank You dear parents, for trusting in me, and letting me work whenever I wanted. My family is the one who supported me for what I am today.
When it comes to this Anthology, I would like to start with Thanking the Co-authors, without your help and support, I would have never been able to complete it.

Thank You all of you, for being there. Much Love to all of You. I am glad to see you all standing by me.

Co Authors

Shubham Shah (Founder Flairs and Glairs)
Ishani Agarwal (Co Founder Flairs and Glairs)
1. Shivangi Jaiswal (Compiler)
2. Jyoti Singh Rajput
3. Heena Shaikh Mulla
4. Deepjyoti Chowdhury
5. Shaily Tyagi
6. Subhrajyoti Nanda
7. Mausam Agrawal
8. अनिल विश्वकर्मा
9. Sachin Banoudhiya
10. Mansi Kanungo
11. Pooja Singh
12. Payal Singhal
13. Pragya Verma
14. Aarti Mahala
15. Tathambika
16. Maitreyee
17. Bickey Mandal
18. Adarsh Kumar Priyadarshi
19. Smriti Kumari
20. Yash Ojha
21. Avi Srivastava
22. Neha Singhania
23. Ritika Sharma
24. Saloni Santosh Gawas
25. Oke Damilola Deborah
26. Khushbu Rathore
27. Sanya Khanna

28.Ekta Pankaj Bathija
29.Vanshika Gupta
30.Parwana Bibi
31.Reshmi Vernekar
32.Atul Kumar
33.Samikhya Swain
34.Dulgach Pooja Singh
35.Muskan Sachdeva
36.Prachi Gupta
37.Saurabh Rajput
38.Pragya Kapil
39.Anmol Chugh Dildard
40.Siya Golani
41.Ujjwal Shree
42.Amita Prabhakar
43.Lokesh Upadhyay
44.Ashwini Kumar Singh
45.Richa Gurudas Mayenkar
46.Parul Sunder
47.Lakshman Mulchandani
48.Riya Srivastava
49.Ayesha Rajpal
50.Shobha Rajpal
51.Vedika Agarwal

Shubham Shah

(Founder- Flairs and Glairs)

Shubham Shah, entrepreneur at "Flairs & Glairs" a brand with dynamics in events organizing and cultural educational pan INDIA, He is a 26yr. old guy who recently has entered, the digital platform of imprinting emotions. He has initiated with his own open mic platform to help budding poets and aspiring writers under his brand named as "Teekhe Zasbaaat"

He is a commerce graduate from Bhagalpur City of Bihar.

He says Writing has impersonated him since childhood and he has now been writing for over a decade!

Cooking, on the other hand, is his passion! He also mentions, trying out new things just tickles him!

When asked sir, Why SPICY EMOTIONS?

He smiled and added, "agar jasbaat teekhe na ho toh wo jasbaat kaha" Spices are all that blends! So do his words!

As a chef, he presents to you his dish! Hot and freshly served! Taste it! Feel it! Enjoy it! You can also find his writing in the Solo book "Teekhe Zasbaaat" and 70+ anthologies. With his passion to explore opportunities across Platforms he is working with keen devotion and We wish him all the very best for his future ventures
Share your reviews on his

INSTAGRAM

@spicy_emotions
@shubham4shah
Or via email on
shubham2shah@gmail.com

To stay tuned to his work and opportunities follow his business Handles

INSTAGRAM   FACEBOOK   YOUTUBE

@flairsandglairs
@teekhezasbaaat

WEBSITE:

https://flairsandglairs.in/
https://flairsandglairs.com/

Ishani Agarwal

(Co Founder- Flairs and Glairs)

Ishani Agarwal
Born and brought up in Kolkata, she has done her schooling and college from here itself. She is doing her post-graduation at the moment. Ishani loves talking to people around, and is excited for this new beginning of hers! Been a Compiler for 35+ Anthologies, and in the process for more, also, co-authored in 100+ Anthologies, Ishani is very Happy with how her life is turning out now!
Insta handle: Ishani_agarwal_quotes

Shivangi Jaiswal

(Compiler)

Shivangi Jaiswal is a Content Writer from Kolkata. Project Head & Coordinator at "Flairs & Glairs" brand with dynamics in events organizing and cultural educational pan INDIA. Organiser at "The Glittering Fables" Writing Community. She is a B.Com Honours graduate. Certified in Stocks & Short Selling as well as Certified in Digital Marketing Been a keen student, she has recently been Certified for learning Spanish Language..She loves to bring smiles and happiness to many faces, so she is into social service. Shivangi has also done her Diploma in painting, drawing and all kinds of clay making, craft works. Traveler, Teacher, Meditator, Dancer, Singer,

Instrument Player. She loves to play guitar and harmonium. Been a public speaker she has taken part in many events and nailed it. Also been a great Advisor to many. Sports freak of Swimming and Badminton with a passion so strong. Since, past one year she has started her writing journey. She writes so that many people can connect with their stories and get positive hopes. She thinks " Every story is unique so embrace yourself to the best".She is a writer by day and a reader by night. Been a Complier of 20+ Anthologies, and in process for more, also Co- authored 60+ anthologies. Shivangi is an old soul with young eyes, a vintage heart, and a beautiful mind."

You can follow her work:

Instagram

@the_knockingvibe

@house_of_compilations

You Complete Me.

You Complete Me.
Never ever I thought of falling in love again.
Now that you are here, I have no fear.
Because I knew I'd truly found my one and only love
of my life.
Your mesmerizing voice saying "I Love You" Makes
me skip a beat.
Your sparkling eyes, the way they stare at me.
Feels like the stars shining at night.
Seeing your soft pink lips, gives me a thought of
kissing you.
My safe place in your arms
Such a blissful moment.
From all the times, holding each other
You have comforted me to ease away the pain.
From being together in all the good and bad times.
Hoping our love stays like a magic.
For as long as you love me.
I'll love you always.

True Love...

Love is pure.
Love is limitless.
But who says love is only meant for lovers?
The purest love is the relation of a child and mother, who carries
the child in her womb for 9 months with care, suffering from all
the problems but still smiling.
Whatever the situation may be she will be always standing by your side.
She would sit starved the whole day waiting for you to eat.
Mom loves is greater than all the relations.
In today's world people say True Love only exists between lovers.
Is it so?
Does love means making and breaking.
Now a day's love is not about trust but all about attractions.
Leaving them alone, depressed, fighting, hating.
But in all this we forget to love the purest ones.
Our true love which is our parents.
Love your parents no matter what,
Because they are our Super Heroes who will never leave our hand
No matter what the circumstance is.
Love you my super heroes.

Wish List...

Night full of stars.
Under the Stars. You & I
Holding hands laying, watching
beauty of the night.

Eyes meeting each other
Disclosing all our wishes to the sky.
The stars light reflecting our smiles
As you wrapped me in your arms.

A spark lit between us
Not knowing what will happen next.
I can feel the warmth of your heart
I feel safe with you.

I don't care about my weakness
Because you're my biggest strength.
I don't fear about my scars,
I'll show you all mine.

Feeling the deep loves of yours.
Under the sky, You & I

Jyoti Singh Rajput

Jyoti Singh Rajput is a banker by profession and marks the ink, as her passion. She believes, the pen holded with passion, has power to bring change and it even emote the emotions, that can't be verbally exchanged and are left unsaid. She is also a lyricist, a nature lover, an enthusiast contributing to welfare works and urges all to help those who needs, as she says, we are human for good deeds. A multilingual and a promising poet, Jyoti Singh Rajput has worked in many books of different genres. She is a basket of masterpieces and her poetry sheds stories, some of love and the memories, some of those tinch and the waving worries, some of life and it's theories. You can follow her on instagram @ the_frozen_flame_2801, and on yourquote @ Jyoti - the frozen flame for her more write ups

"Love" A Treasure

Love Not Always Meant To Be Forever
At Times It Happens In A Moment
And That Moment Becomes
A Memory To Treasure...

The Emotions Unveiled

They Keep Talking In Eyes
And The Exchange Of Emotions Happened
That Once Were, Hidden Inside...

Her "Love Story"

Once She Had A Friend,
Now Called, Her Dear Husband...

Heena Shaikh Mulla

Heena Shaikh Mulla is from Pune,currently residing in Karnataka.

She's from an ICSE background,graduated from Pune University(MSC Computer Science). She's the author of 'Technical Desserts' and also hold a Vajra record for the same. Besides being a college topper,She likes drawing henna,teaching and fantasizes about Polar Bears.

She's a charming personality who expresses her thoughts in the form of Poetry and Shayri and currently she's compiling books as well.

I Too Had A Love Story

I Too Had A Love Story,
 Where I Fell For Him,
When We First Met In The Gym,
But According To Him It Was Contrary.

Instead Of A Rose,
He Approached Me With A Prop,
And Asked Me To Hop,
To Which I Couldn't Oppose.

We Shared A Nice Bond,
Until One Fine Day He Had To Depart,
 It Did Tore Me Apart,
But We Left With A Hope To Again Meet In Some Other
Pond.

Deepjyoti Chowdhury

Deepjyoti Chowdhury embraces reading and writing as her escape from the real world as well as a window to it. She is a strong believer of Christ and Karma. Written in 100+ anthologies, she is the author of "Heartfelt musings" and "The staircase to freedom". Her main aim is to heal people and make them smile through her art of writing. You can follow her on Instagram at dj_writes_to_heal .

Carved In The Pages Of My Soul

Your name is written on the pages of my soul,
Carved permanently capturing it whole.
You would soon be near, my heart I console;
Loving you endlessly is my motive and goal.

Carved your name in my heart forever,
Will pass this beautiful journey together.
Each moments we spent, I remember;
To explain it all I need love interpreter.

The ring on my finger I endlessly adore,
To visualize that beautiful day and restore.
With manuscripts my love hence I secure,
The spark is ever glowing just like before.

No love story is simple and sorted,
So has mine been a little distorted.
But assembling all the pieces scattered,
Loving you forever I hence move forward.

Shaily Tyagi

She is Shaily Tyagi, a born writer.

She is always ready to face challenges and gives her best in every field.

She is a compiler, loves to compile different feelings of different hearts.

Here she is with her beautiful poem, hope all will love to read.

<u>याद है</u>

याद है तुमको वह गली वह चौबारे,
जहां हम हुए थे तुम्हारे और तुम हुए हमारे!
वह घूमना लेकर हाथों में हाथ ,
चलते थे राहों में हम यूं साथ-साथ !
दुनिया की तो जैसे फिक्र ही कहां थी ,
औरों की तो क्या खुद की भी कदर कहां थी!
बस तुम थे और तुम्हारा प्यार था,
तुम बिन ना कहीं चेन ना कहीं करार था !
देख के तुमको ही सुकून था ,
ना जाने कैसा वह इश्क का जुनून था!
याद है तुमको वह गली वह चौबारा ,
जहां मिल ना सके तुम हमसे दोबारा!

Subhrajyoti Nanda

Subhrajyoti Nanda is a 17 years old student from Odisha,a published co author in many anthologies,a district level debator, a state level essay writing winner and also loves to host, dance and sing.She feels, writing exhibits his beats and she was inspired by her father,who is himself a poet and the ink inspires her in her own ways.She has received many awards in these fields and aims to shape the society with her positive perspective and unconditional kindness.

Threads Of Love!

The huge tree stands straight with solitude and being home to none. His lushy leaves explains the little buds about their blossoming. It is autumn and the birth of winter arises the birds to cheer in the greenery and they gets to know one of the best love story of the living planet is going to happen.

In the highest depths of the sky,the symphonic sound of the birds thrill every body and mind of the individuals.From the greenest canopies,the ivory billed woodpecker cackles and finds the huge tree as her new destination.Without interrupted thoughts yet with buffering beats, the bird starts pecking the tree all of a sudden with all her potential.And for the first time ever,the enormous body of the huge tree swells with unexpected torment.

The bird with much patience and endurance continues pecking and speaks, "Your smooth bark is as soft as those kissed cheeks of a teenager and I admire them much. "The tree looks frustrated ,with intermittent pain and pangs and he continues to consider the bird as a sinner and starts loathing more.

Continuous days and nights, the bird goes on carving out the poor tree and he stands with annoyance and irresistible pain. The drillings of the bird echoes in the citadel of the woodland and the tree sobs to his last. Other way,she is silent yet whispers every words of her love and passion and to stay near him as always ever. She swears to stay

 the closest to him and to heal his unwanted pain; she is giving him at the present.

After some time, the construction of the vast hole finishes,slashing the constant agony of the tree to the end.

Still,unknown of her passionate love and admiration towards him, he is indignant and stays quiet.

And at the precise time,the bird starts pouring out her pearly tears and speaks,"No doubt, I hurt you much to the fullest.My hurtful beak instil waves of pessimistic feelings in you. But trust me a little, I never want to do so, yet out of the search of permanent shelter, I was bound to hurt you that harder. I know,you are the embodiment of enormity and benignity and you'll surely come forward to accept me to live with you forever.Indeed,I want to feel you,both from inside and outside,staying safe with you as long as I'm alive."

Her confession is true enough to smoulder the tender heart of the huge tree and he is contented all ever.

As always ever, LOVE has the most ecstatic charmness and the same happens between the duo.

And the end,the huge tree murmers the best lines ever, "Though we are restless; yet I love you."

And the woody woodpecker replies with much shyness and happiness,"You love me more."

Mausam Agrawal

She is a 22 year old girl from Nepal and has completed her graduation from Kolkata.She loves writing poems,shayaris and stories.

Ishq Chori Chori

Mohalle mai meri
Aaya naya sa chera tha
Huye sab deewana jiske
Woh chup chup ke mujhpe marta tha

Ek raat kuch hua yun
Ki aankhein mil gayi usse
Aur mili aisi ki phir hati hi nahi
Woh dil mai kuch yun bas gaya
Jaise batke musafir ko raasta naya mil gaya
Main beparwah sa tha
Uske aane se samhalne laga tha

Ishq Ho Gaya Tha Izhaar Baki Tha

Woh din mujhe yaad hai
Jab woh mulakat thi
Izhaar ke raat ki
Chupke se mile the
Karni guftgu jo khaas thi
Chand ki chandani bhi sharma gayi
Dekh kar uska chera
Huyi puri kahani ishq ki
Jo hua tha chori chori

Aaj phir aaya hai naya chand kiska mohalle mai
Phir ek nayi kahani likhi jayegi
Ishq ki chori chori

अनिल विश्वकर्मा

लेखक को श्री अनिल कुमार विश्वकर्मा के नाम से जाना जाता है, वे देश की राजधानी दिल्ली से सम्बन्ध रखते हैं। उनकी स्नातक की शिक्षा दिल्ली विश्वविद्यालय से हुई है तथा वर्तमान में वे एक प्रतिष्ठित संगठन में कार्यरत हैं। वे एक गम्भीर व ज़िम्मेदार युवक होने के साथ-साथ कर्तव्यनिष्ठ और पारिवारिक व्यक्ति भी हैं। अपने जीवन के दैनिक कार्यों में व्यस्त रहते हुए भी वे अपनी लेखन रुचि को जीवित रखते हैं। अपने स्नातकोत्तर के दौरान ही उनमें लेखन की रुचि उत्पन्न हो गई थी, किंतु इस कला को भौतिक स्वरूप देने में उन्हें कुछ समय लगा। उनके लेखन की प्रेरणा व स्रोत उनकी प्रिय जीवनसंगिनी है। वे थोड़े अल्पभाषी है किंतु कलम के माध्यम से वे अपनी बात कहना जानते हैं। वे अपनी रचनाओं और लेखनी के माध्यम से आप लोगों से जुड़ना चाहते हैं तथा साथ ही साथ यह भी कामना करते हैं कि आप लोगों का प्रोत्साहन व स्नेह भी उन्हें भरपूर मिले क्योंकि वे इस क्षेत्र में अभी नवीन हैं परंतु इस यात्रा में और आगे तक जाने की इच्छा रखते हैं।

Instagram: Www.instagram.com/anil0287

<u>नज़र आशिकाना।</u>

ये नज़र क़ातिलाना, अंदाज़ आशिक़ाना,

जब की है मोहब्बत, तो फिर क्या शरमाना।

मेरी सासों में आप बसे हो, ज़रा गौर फरमाना,

मेरे जिस्म से मिल जाना, मेरी रुह में समाना,

वो धीरे से आपका कुछ कहना, और पलट जाना,

आना ही पड़ेगा इस बार, नहीं चलेगा कोई बहाना।

जब लूँगा अपनी बाहों में, तो मुझसे ना घबराना,

हटा कर अपना घूँघट, चाँद-सा चेहरा मुझे दिखाना।

ये नज़र क़ातिलाना, अंदाज़ आशिक़ाना,

कितना हमें चाहते हो, ज़रा हमें भी बताना।

होठों से कुछ तो बोलिये, दिल में ना कुछ छुपाना,

यूँ आपका पल में रूठना, और फिर मेरा मनाना।

इतनी सारी बातें वो आपका हंसना और हंसाना,

कभी कुछ कहूँ मैं, कभी आप का कुछ सुनाना।

चलो मिल-कर हम, बनाये कोई नया अफसाना,

मुझे अकेला छोड़ कर, तुम कहीं ना जाना।

ये नज़र क़ातिलाना, अंदाज़ आशिक़ाना,

कितना प्यार करते हो, ज़रा हमें भी बताना।

कब से कर रहा हूँ इंतज़ार, एक बार मिल जाना,

पकड़ लो तुम सवारी, और हो जाओ जी रवाना।

मुझसे फिर मिलके, तुम जुदा ना हो जाना,

मेरा इस दुनिया में, नहीं है और कोई ठिकाना।

याद में तेरी जलता है, तेरा ये परवाना,

जैसे बिन तेल के, किसी दिये का फड़फड़ाना।

ये नज़र क़ातिलाना, अंदाज़ आशिक़ाना,

कितना याद करते हो, ज़रा हमें भी बताना।

Sachin Banoudhiya

He is a student of Bsc
A Struggling Writter now Started Getting so many platforms
He Loves to do Audio Poetries & video Editing .
He's a Publish Co - author in so many Anthologies

Dream Girl

Kuch Esi Hogi Meri Dream Girl
Jiski Height kuch bhi ho Doesn't matter
Bs itni ho ki meri dil ki dhadkano ko sun ske
Weight itna jisko Uthakr pura world Tour Krwa Sku
Aankhe Esi jinme Doob Jaane ko dil chahe
Julfe Esi jinme kho jaane Ko Man kre
Cute To m use bana he dunga

Qualification itni Jo meri Dil ki Baate pd ske.
Name kuch bhi ho Chalega
Bas Surname Mera Lagwadunga
Address kahi bhi rhe
Jo bhale He sbse mile
Bs uske Dil m hai rhu
Jo mere saare nakhre uthaye
Or roz kuch acha banakr khilaye
roZ subh apni mithi aawaz se uthaye
Duniya ki bheed m
Mujh sang slow motion m bhaage
Wo mere dreams ke Peeche or
M uske aage
Pagalpanti m kre jo mera Support

Kuch esi hogi meri dream girl

Mansi Kanungo

मेरा नाम मानसी कानूनगो है, मैं इंदौर (मध्यप्रदेश) से हूं। मैं 19 वर्ष की हूं , लिखना मेरा पेशा नहीं मेरी आदत है।

(1)

दिल की बात मैं तुझे बताने से घबराता हूं,

अक्सर मैं तुझे देखने के लिए घंटो ही धूप में खड़ा रह जाता हूं,

मैं बस तुझे निहारने के लिए तो तेरी गलियों में बार बार आता जाता हूं,

अब कैसे बताऊं तुझे कि

तेरी वो प्यारी सी मुस्कराहट पर ही तो मैं हर बार मर जाता हूं........।।

(2)

Uska diya vo jhumka ab yaad ane laga hai,

Pr ab vo kisi or se dil lagane laga hai,

Pehle toh vo hak se sirf mera tha,

Ab lagta hai... Vo kisi or ki gali jane laga hai.....

(3)

ना तो मंज़िल का ठिकाना है और ना ही रास्तों का पता, कहीं जीने का आसरा मिल जाए.....

बस अनजानों की तरह चले जा रहे हैं, पता नहीं किस मोड़ पर एक और मुसाफ़िर मिल जाए.....।।

Pooja Singh

Pooja Singh stays in Mumbai the place she loves to be.
She's pursuing dentistry as a profession.
But besides that she likes to express her emotions and thoughts through poems.
She writes on many genre specially on women empowerment.
She prefers writing her own creation.
And hope to reach hearts of the readers.
She believes in philosophy that "Happiness is an inside job".

In Your Eyes.

In your eyes , I'm alive.
always felt magical the way you look in my sight.
Our story its like stars falling from the sky.
like the shades of rose pink on my cheeks.
when you hold my hands there's thunder in my spine.
you brought me sunshine when i was in rain.
you brought me laughter when i went through pain.
When I see in the mirror of the image of you and I.
that's just what i want for the rest of the life.

Payal Singhal

Payal Singhal, a commerce graduate. She is a bibliophile who believes that there is magic in writing, which gives her the liberty to express herself, and most importantly, given the privilege to become soliloquy. She writes to bring a positive impact on society, and she knew pen and paper never judge but give a solution and peace every time.

Insta id: @psinscriptions

Baatein Nahi Hoti Aajkal

Mile jab hum pehli baar usko, woh yaar hua
Baatein krte krte na jaane kab pyaar hua

Chhat par jate hi uski ek jhalak pane ko
Ek pal toh kabhi do pal ka intzaar hua

Milen usse hum phir chup chup ke
Na jaane aankhon hi aankhon mein kb ikrar hua

Mulaqaatein chalti rahi unke saath issi tarah
Na jaane kaise kisi ka itna gehra rang mujhpar sawaar hua

Bichad gaye do aashiq phir se ek hokar
Dil tut ke ek se do phir do se chaar hua

Baatein nahi hoti aajkal unse par ek sawaal hai humara
Mere jaane ke baad Kya phir kahin kabhi kisi se aisa pyaar
hua?

Pragya Verma

Pragya Verma is born and raised in Prayagraj, Uttar Pradesh. She is currently pursuing Bachelor's in Computer Application. She is a poet and a writer.

क्या यह इश्क नहीं?

तुझे देखने के लिए छत पर आना,
और तुझे देखते ही मुस्कुरा कर छुप जाना,
आंखों से आंखों का मिलना,
बिना कहे, बिना सुने सब कुछ समझ जाना।

मन ही मन बस ये सोचना,
कि काश तेरी मेरी छत बगल में होती।
और उस पर तेरा मुझे देख कर मुस्कुराना,
इतना ही काफी था मेरे लिए इस दिल को हारना।

तेरे इशारों को चुटकी में समझ जाना,
हां, आता है मुझे तेरे बिना कुछ बोले सब समझ जाना।

तेरा मिलने को कहना और मेरा घबराना,
फिर तेरा मुझसे रूठ जाना,
इन सब में कब इश्क हो गया कुछ पता ही न चला,
तुमको अपना मान लिया है हमने, यह तुम्हे क्या पता।

(2)

हर पल तेरे बारे में सोचना,
छत पर जाने के बहाने ढूंढना,
तुझे बस एक बार देख लूं इतना ही चाहना,
क्या यह इश्क नहीं? खुद से यही सवाल करना।

किसी अंजाने से इतना गहरा रिश्ता जुड़ जाना,
कि उसके न होने पर सब कुछ अधूरा लगना,
तुम ही बताओ क्या तुमको भी होता है ऐसा?
या मैं ही पागल हूं तुम्हारे पीछे बेवजह।।

Tathambika

She is girl with big dreams, a mba scholar & just express what she feels. She is from dhanbad, Jharkhand
For more follow in Insta- tathu895(crazy thoughts)

Mohalle Vala Ishq

Mohalle ki vo gali, chhat mein milane ka bahana yaad hai,
Vah Mohabbat, vo deewangi abhi bhi vo jamana yad hai...
Gajab ka andaaz tha tumhare mohabaat krne ka,
tumhari ek jhalak ki chah main roj ungaliyon se gujarta tha...
Mere har pal mein Tum maujud thi,
tabhi to tumhare Dil ke Dhadkan se gujarta tha....
Ek rishte k liye kayi rishte takk pae rakhe the maine,
apne ishq k liye roj sholo se gujarta tha....
Meri chhat uski balcony ko barso se janti hai,
bharosa nahi hai to puchlo usse hamare ishq ki sakshi vo khud
ko ajjvi manti hai...
Sabke dimag ki batti jal rhi thi,tera mera chakkr h mohalle mae
assi baat chal thi...
Hazaro phere lagaye the maine tumhare galiyon ke,
Koi kismat vala tumhe saat phero mae le gya tha.....
Uss mohalle ka, ganit mae sbse kamjor lrka, tere sath bitaye
hue ek-ek pal bakhubi hisaab rakhta tha....
Uss mohalle vale pyar ka vi ajeeb fasana tha, char ghar ki duri
aur bich mae sara zamana tha.....

Maitreyee

She is Maitreyee. Don't go by her age since she can bemuse you with her words. She is bubbly,
scintilating and ambitious. She holds expertise in story telling , micro tales and also knows to weave words into beautiful poetries! She is a big foodie amd also loves cooking.

आज फिर ~

आज फ़िर उन गलियों में विहार किया,

जिसमे तुम और मैं हुआ करते थे।

आज फ़िर उन पलों को याद किया,

जिसमे तुम और मैं जीया करते थे।

आज फिर उन घरों का दीदार किया,

जिसमे तुम और मैं रहा करते थे।

आज फिर उस मुस्कुराहट को महसूस किया

जिसकी वजह हमेशा तुम हुआ करते थे।

आज फिर आईने के सामने कुछ अटपटा किया

जिसे देखकर तुम हमेशा हँसा करते थे।

आज फिर उस सुकून का एहसास किया

जो तुम अपनी प्यार भरीं बातों से मुझे दिया करते थे।

आज फिर तुम्हारे वादों को याद किया

जो करते करते तुम थका ना करते थे।

आज फिर उस सच से सामना हुआ है

जिसे कबूल करने से तुम मना किया करते थे।

आज फिर अपनी किस्मत से पर्दा किया

जिसमे शामिल होने की बात तुम हमेशा किया करते थे।

चलो अब बहुत हुआ, अब और नहीं कर पाऊँगी ,

थक गयीं हूँ बहुत, अब और नहीं चल पाऊँगी,

छोड़ जा रहीँ हुँ तुम्हारी यादों को इन्हीं गलियों में,

इश्क़ हमारा नायाब था ये तो हमें खबर है

पर कम्बख्त वक़्त से भी क्या ही गिला करें

लाज़मी है की ये तो बेसबर है!

Bickey Mandal

He is Bickey Mandal from Jharkhand. Now he is in the last semester of his graduation from B.B.M.K.U Dhanbad with English Honours. With his poetries he trying to connect himself with others. He is passionate about his works because he love what he do. He have a stedy source of motivations that drives him to do his best. You can contact him through instagram at @bickey_ki_ankahi_baatein

E-mail- bickeymandal91@gmail.com

I Am Nothing Without You

Love is not sacrifice anything,
but winning everyone's heart.
I want to hold your hand tightly
When I scared,
But I'm just afraid of your leaving.

I think I am happy without you.
But I can't be happy,
because I am happy only with you.

Without you I am nothing.
I am as like as a blank page.

I can't complete my love story.
I can't complete my love letters too.
I can't imagine my life without you.
Because
you came never ever to forever in my life.

If you have decided to
make the descision of separating,
Otherwise you were the nearest to me.

I can't forgive you, But forget you.
And regret myself, For my mistakes.

Adarsh Kumar Priyadarshi

Adarsh Kumar Priyadarshi is a school going boy form a small town called Hajipur, Bihar. His father servers the nation in Indian Army. And his mother is a housemarker. He is co-author of 40+ anthology As he is proud to be the son of a loyal army man so he too wants to do something great for his mother-land. As he has a great zeal in medical field so he is currently even struggling with his journey to reach his destination, his goal i.e. to be a renowned doctor. He always thanks his parents, teachers, friend and God for what he is now.

 His debut, book will be launched soon.

You can follow him on Instagram (@adarsh_priyadarshi_03)

(1)

I'm not just falling in love with you. I'm falling in to you. you're an ocean, and I'm falling in, drowning in the depths of who you are, like you said, it's a scary in a way, but it's also more amazing thing I've ever experienced. You're the most amazing thing I've ever experienced.

Pure Love

When you smile because of someone,
It's a special felling.

But when you cry for someone,

It's love.

Smriti Kumari

Smriti kumari is student by profession,writer by passion.she lives in New Delhi,india.She is 2nd year student, pursuing bsc(h) maths from Rajdhani college,Delhi University. She is an optimistic, passionate, inquisitive and hardworking.she has worked for many anthologies as co-author.The pen is a strong weapon for her to portray her feelings.she loves to write in her spare time.Friends and parents are the biggest support of her.let's enjoy her writing and shower your love.

ये इश्क़ पारदर्शी!

क्या उनसे नज़रों से नज़रें मिलना लाजमी था,

क्या उनका इस कदर मुस्कुराना लाजमी था?

करनी थी बेहिसाब बातें उनसे,

फिर क्या उनका मुड़कर जाना लाजमी था?

क्या शाम ढले मुझे बालकनी में और

उनका छत पर आना लाजमी था।

धीरे धीरे दिल की तारों को जोड़,

मुझे यूं मदहोश कर जाना लाजमी था।

इशारों में सबकुछ कह जाना,

फिर धीरे- धीरे नज़रें चुराना।

फिर क्या उनका ये इश्क़ छुपाना लाजमी था।

अपने रंगों से रंगकर,ख्यालों में मुझे डुबोकर,

क्या उनका,

इश्क़ की कश्ती को ऐसे बहाना लाजमी था।

क्या उनका इस कदर मुस्कुराना लाजमी था?

Yash Ojha

He is "YASH OJHA" son of 'Dr. Ram Sahay Ojha' and 'Mrs. Usha Ojha' , born and raised in Ayodhaya, UP. He completed his schooling from Udaya Public School and now is pursuing Graduation in Arts(hons.) with English currently. He has a Degree in Hacking field as well. Writing was not a profession but somehow became passion for him. Now he has completed his own 30+ Poetries as well. The flow of his words seemed effortless, and before he knew about it. It had grown beyond this many poetries which was on his hands.

He received so much encouragement and positive feedbacks from his parents and others and then he found that he shouldn't stop writing.

"Love of Lovebirds"...

My life is just like a body without a soul in it,
It is this only possible because of you otherwise my life was
just like a person who only Feels and breathes Air but can't
Express his emotions of love to their love birds,

We fall in each other by our limits of love and happiness,

We came to each other by the vibes of our people's and grace
of many well wishers,

We come to be next to each other because of our love of many
life,

We can give the world our prints of shining of love that show
and connects us to our love till last soul....

Avi Srivastava

He is an engineering student aimed to make his name in computer world...
Poetry is not only is his hobby but also a way to express his feelings....

वो तेरा आना...

छत पर तेरा यूँ रोज कपड़े सुखाना....
देख मुझे शर्मा कर छुप जाना....
मेरा रोज कसरत के बहाने तुझे निहारना....
बयां न कर सकता मेरे जीवन मे तेरा आना....

वो तेरे छत पर जान कर पतंग गिरना....
कागज के जहाज पर दिल की बातें लिखना....
अनजाना सा हैं ये एहसास मुश्किल हैं तम्हें समझाना....
तेरा तोलिये से बारिशें आज़ाद करना करे मुझे दीवाना....

Neha Singhania

Hello,introducing Neha Singhania. She is Pursuing CS and a good dancer and a dance tutor too.Writing is her passion, and she want to be a good known writter. she always try to write on undefined feelings. she is having her own instagram page @ dil-e-ehsasss

पहला प्यार

रहती है मेरे पड़ोस में,
चार कदम बस दूर में।
आती भी है मेरे घर वो,
बहुत प्यारी से सज कर वो।

उसे देख मेरी धड़कन बढ़कर,
करने लगती है कुछ कुछ गड़बड़।
चुप चुपके निहारता हूँ उसको
सामने बोल ना पता कुछ उसके
पर आइना समझ खूब बाते करता हूँ उससे।
रहती है मेरे पड़ोस में।

कई चक्कर लगाता उसके घर के,
बस उसकी एक नज़र पाने को।
उसकी एक मुस्कुराहट में मैं फिदा हूँ,
उसकी एक आवाज़ में मैं खड़ा हूँ ।
रहती है मेरे पड़ोस में।

मेरे ये पेहले प्यार का चर्चा है,
उसको छोड़ पूरे मोहल्ले को पता हैं
हमारी तो कभी दोस्ती भी नही हुई
फिर भी सपने बहुत आगे के देखता हूँ
पडोस वाला पहला प्यार
दिल मे बसाये रखता हूँ।

जनाब!
मोहब्बत के किस्से तो बहुत होते है
पर मेरी ये मोहब्बत कुछ ऐसी है
जो ना ही आगे बढ़ती है
ना ही कभी खत्म ही होती है।

Ritika Sharma

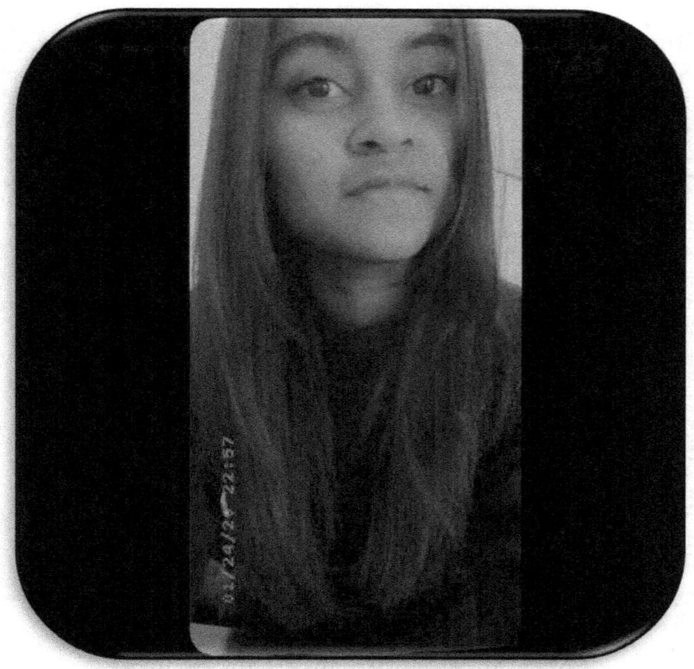

Ritika Sharma is pursing bachelors of mass communication and journalism .she has keen interest in various things like painting , sketching , dancing , acting , making digital content and of course writing . she has written a number of poems , shayari and other things . she has keen interest in writing and describing things uniquely . come lets explore her thought over a write up in this book .

"सही"

हर कोई कहता है "सही" करो , "सही" लोगो के साथ रहो , "सही"
राह पकडो़
पर यह "सही" है क्या ?
उसका पता कैसे लगता है ?
क्या आप "सही" है , पूरे ?
क्या में "सही" हूँ , पूरी ?
क्या में "सही" नहीं ?
क्या आप भी गलत हो ?
क्या यह "सही" के चक्कर, में हम अक्सर गलत कर देते है ?
या फिर गलत भी "सही" है ?
या फिर गलत ही "सही" है ?
या फिर "सही" कुछ है ही नहीं ?
या फिर "सही" सिर्फ गलत का एक रूप है ?
क्या "सही" करना बहुत जरूरी है ?
क्या "सही" नहीं करेंगे तो चलेगा ?
या फिर "सही" इतना जरुरी है ,
की गलत का नामो, निशान मिट जाये ?
लेकिन अगर गलत चला गया तो फिर "सही" का पता लगेगा ?
क्या "सही" गलत के बगैर भी "सही" है ?
या शायद, "सही" तब तक "सही" है जब तक गलत भी ज़िंदा है ?
अगर गलत मर गया तो "सही" कैसे ज़िंदा रह सकता है ?
या फिर "सही" गलत के बिना भी जिंदा है ?
"सही" का पता चल जाए तो , ज़िन्दगी क्या है ?
"सही" का पता चल जाए तो , ज़िन्दगी क्या है ?
सिर्फ "सही" रह जाए तो

"सही" का क्या पता है ?
गलत है ज़िंदा तभी तो ,
"सही" का भी पता है ?
गलत भी हो करते तभी
तो "सही" की भी एक राह है |

Saloni Santosh Gawas

She is student. This year she completed her 12th std and pursuing education for her undergraduate course.

For her writing is living her passion. She started writing from young age, due to some reason took a drop of few years.

As passion can't remain hidden for long, life gave rebirth for her passion. She has written many poems, some qoutes and short stories.

When Love Exist in Pure Form

A day that opened
Like a big beautiful ocean
I heard the waves singing
Yes, they were singing

The sand built castles
Wind blew it slowly on us
A long walk on the shore
Holding your hand like never to go

A silent evening
Sitting on the shore
Sand carried our footprints
As a proof of our Love

Wave arrived, a huge one
Vanished them, all of a sudden
Holding my hand you smilingly said
That wave will keep, it forever Alive...

Gift to Heart

The constant feeling of togetherness
A colourful painting
Which is totally flawless..

The person who fill our life
With all the happiness..
Is the relationship
Which is just endless..

A special person which everyone has
A lifetime promise which they share
The journey doesn't start together
But with same destination both are blessed...

Top of all is
Existence of unconditional love
Proper definition of trust and care
That's the love which never fades...

Oke Damilola Deborah

Oke Damilola is a 19 year old Nigerian writer.She started writing as a hobby in the year 2016 and she is very excited to have some of her work published in this book.

Love Sonnet

The gum of your love is glued on the surface of my heart.
Intoxicated by your affection I'm filled within.
Care and caressing my body never lack.
Fear and despair melt away with you around.
Let us write a tale of our beautiful love,let us take our
adventure to the peak,You,my love will always be my pick !

In You

You are like an air,
In you hold my breath,
My breath for love.
You're like a quench,
In you hold my thirst,
My thirst for torch.
You're like a bed,
In you hold my rest,
My rest of mind and body.
You're like a food,
With you I have the strength,
The strength to live everyday.

Real Meaning

To love is Longing, satisfaction. Undefined feelings captured in an epitome of care.Dancing to the sound of a beautiful song with all happiness,that's what it is.

Touch,attraction.A very strong conviction with no doubt, looking straight at your desire with no turning back.

Truth,trust.No deceit is found no matter how careful you look.

Loyalty, forgiveness.Letting go of the past with the presence to embrace.

To love is looking beyond the invisible and focusing on what is captured inside.

To love is to see beyond weaknesses.

Khushbu Rathore

An independent soul who likes to read, write, pants and design. A girl who, through poetry, expresses her feelings and enjoys comfort.

B. Ed is very talented girl with getting education. A proud girl from Pali district of Rajasthan receives her education during the day and most of her time in the night gives her time to the writing work. She is Khusbu Rathore and is delighted to be a part of this anthology

Instagram =@khushburathore1913

इश्क - ए- मोहल्ला

अजीब है इश्क का मोहल्ला अपना

कोई शायर बना , कोई उसकी शायरी

वो मोहल्ले की छत वाला इश्क करना है मुझे

जहाँ वो इमोजी की जगह अपना चेहरा बनाये

अजीब सी बस्ती मे ठिकाना है मेरा

जहा लोग मिलते कम है, झांकते ज्यादा है

प्यार ऐसा ना करो की पूरा मोहल्ला देखे

प्यार कुछ ऐसे करो की

पूरा मोहल्ला तुमसे कुछ सीखे

कभी मेरी तुमसे मुलाकात होगी

कुछ अनकही सी बात होगी

हम पूछेंगे हाल तुम्हारा

तुम्हारी आंखे नम और साँसों से बात होगी

आज उसकी गली से गुज़रते हुए

इन भटके हुए कदमों को राह मिल गयी है

मेरी गालियों से तुम भटके हो

रास्ता मुझे नजर नहीं आ रहा है

जिस गली में

यूँ देखते है गौर के अब तो मोहल्ले के सभी,
हमने भी पीछे की गली से आना जाना कर दिया

यूँ गुनगुनाते है सभी किस्से हमारे हर जगह,
इस अनकही सी कहानी को तराना कर दिया

फिर आज पूछा माँ ने हमसे क्यों हो इतने बेख़बर
हमने भी फिर से तबीयत का बहाना कर दिया

वो देख के यूँ मुस्कुराए हमको गली के सामने
दीवाना हमे वो कर गए
और दुश्मन ज़माना कर दिया

Sanya Khanna

Sanya is someone who always manages to create a positive aura around her. She is constantly smiling without complaining much about the difficulties. She is confident in whatever she does and is very hardworking. She has never learnt to give up in life. She has a keen interest in writing. She is extremely friendly and manages to work well in a team and that is her greatest strength!

|खुबसूरत एहसास |

प्यार एक एहसास है
जिसका होना बेहद खास है
जिसे मिल जाए वो खुशनसीब है,
वरना इसके बिना तो सारा मोहल्ला गरीब है

वो पहली नज़र , वो पहली मुलाकात
जैसे सावन कि पहली बरसात
भूल ना पाओ जिसे तुम
चाहे दिन हो या रात..

सपने भी अब तो उन्ही के आते है
एक गेहरा राज़ हमें बताते है
दिन भर जिनकी याद सताती है
उनकी एक अवाज़ दिल बहलाती है

दूर हो हम या हो करीब
उनसे मिलना था मेरा नसीब
कितनी रातें गुज़ारी मैंने
करने मे उनसे बातचीत..

आज दिल इस बात को जानता है
और हर आशिक भी इसको मानता है
कि प्यार एक एहसास है
जिसका होना बेहद खास है!

Ekta Pankaj Bathija

एकता. पी .बठीजा का जन्म बैंगलोर में हुआ है। वो साइरा के नान
से भी लिखती है।उन्होंने १० साल की उम्र से लिखना शुरू किया
था।वक़्त के साथ - साथ उनके लिखने का तरीका तथा स्तर भी
बदलता गया। उनके हिसाब से लिखना हमारे मन के भावनाओ को
दर्शाता है ।

<u>मोहल्ले वाली</u>

फिर चल रहे गप्पे
फिर चल रहे गप्पे
यारों के संग अपने
चाय की टपरी पे बैठे
मज़े कर रहे सारे।

दोस्तों से चुपके
निगाहें इधर-उधर है भटके
आपके एक दीदार के लिए
न जाने क्या क्या करने पढ़ते।

ठहाकों के शोर में
एक छनक सी आयी
आपके बाजेब की छनक
आप ओर ले आयी।

थमी साँसों से आपको
ढूंढे मेरी निगाहे
उन झुकी पलकों में
हाए दिल हारे हम बेचारे ।

गोल गप्पे की टपरी देख
मन आपका ललचाये
सहेली संग खाती गोल गप्पे
खते मैं मुह बनाए।

परेशान करती जुल्फें
फिर भी न छोड़े गोल गप्पे
खते - खते, तीखे - तीखे
खाती है गोल गप्पे
बच्चो से भी ज़्यादा सुंदर
लगती है उस पल में।

क्या करे बेचारे हम
मोहल्ले वाले है सारे अपने।

Vanshika Gupta

Vanshika Gupta, born and raised in India; 17 years old now. Coming to her goals and career, she don't have any short time goal. All she wants to be is a writer. She wants her words to be the reason behind her success. Had been writing since past 4 years, and would want to carry this occupation forever.

(1)

Koi noor hai tu
Kohinoor hai tu
Paas na sahi,
Hoor sa ehsaas hai tu!

Hamesha Ki Talaash

Hamesha ki talaash mein
Maano aaj kho saa gaya hai
Mohabbat rooh se nahi
Jismo se hone lag gaya hai
Talaash hai uss shaks ki
Dil ibaadat kar raha hai
Hamesha ki talaash mein
Maano aaj kho saa gaya hai !

(3)

Chahe daulat ho, shohrat ho, mohabbat ho, rishte ho ya zindagi,
Moh khatam hote hi khone ka darr bhi kho jaata hai!

Parwana Bibi

Parwana Bibi a little moody and shy girl . She want to see people happy and she is so cute . She is very talented and never give up any situation . Let's see what she write for us.

Mohalle Wala Ishq

Mere cycle ki pahiyon ka dhire dhire gadhna ,
Teri halki si muskan se woh najre jhukana .....

Haye dil to wahin pighal he jata hai moum ki tarha ,
Teri woh nazakat se ankho ka kuch ishara mere taraf karna .....

Ab hum kahan hum rehe gaye hain ,
Tere he to diwane ban chuke hain .....

Tujhe dekhte dekhte woh kisi aur se jake takrana ,
Aur unse muafi mangte mangte tera gum ho jana .....

Fir tujhe dhundte huye paglon sa logon ko puchhte huye firna
,
Fir achanak se tera mere samne aakar khade ho jana .....

Din to wahin ban jata hai tujh se mulaqat kar ke ,
Mano meri zindegi ko jaise bas intezar thha tera he .....

Teri baton se mera dil tujh pe fida hone laga aur tu hasne lagi
thhi ,
Aur fir yeh mausum ki baarish peheli baar milne ko yaadgar
bana gayi .....

Pyar

Pyar do lafzon se ya teen alfaaz se pure nahi hote hain ,
Inhe muqamal karne ko to kabhi kabhi zindegi bhi kam padh jate hain .....

Pyar kisi ke han ya nah se simat nahi jata hai ,
Woh to sacha hota hai aur apni parwan chadh kar dikhata hai .....

Chahe ishq galiyon se suru hua ho ya mohallon se lekin khumar to chadhta he hai ,
Ishq to ishq hota hai woh kahin bhi apna basera bana leta hai .....

Reshmi Vernekar

Reshmi Maheshwar vernekar has completed her Master degree in (hindi language) and currently doing bechular degree in education (b.ed) at pragati women's collge of education at torxem she want to become a teacher her hobbies are reading books,cooking, she also like to do social services

हमारा प्यार

कल तुम एक अजनबी थे लेकिन कब अपने बन गए पता ही नहीं चला ।

आज मैं तुम्हारी चांदनी हूँ तुम मेरा चांद । रख दो तुम्हारा हाथ मेरे हाथों में इस तरह की अपने जीवन में हम सफर बना दो, मुझे तुम्हारे दिल की धड़कन बना दो, तुम्हारे दर्द में हमदर्द बना लो। यह मेरे पहले प्यार की कविता हो तुम, मेरे हर दुआ में हो तुम । तुम्हारी चाहत में इश्क सिखा दिया है । हमारे प्यार का इजहार कैसे करूं? किस से करूं? कि तुम्हारे बिना मैं कैसे बन गई हूँ । किससे कहूं कि मैं तुमसे कितना प्यार करती हूँ ? तुम मेरे दिल की आदत बन गए, इस दिल में सुबह - शाम तुम्हारी हीआवाज सुनती हूँ।

हम दोनों ने मिलकर जिंदगी के सपने देखे थे लेकिन तुम मुस्कुराकर चले गए । अपना बनाना था तुम पराया करके चले गए। मुझे नहीं पता तुम मुझसे क्या सीखे लेकिन हां मैं तुमसे बहुत कुछ सीखी हूँ । मेरे लिए सब कुछ थे तुम लेकिन तुम्हारा यह सबके सामने मुझे पराया करना पसंद ना था मुझे । प्यार में सब कुछ सह लिया मैंने । ना तुम कभी समझपाए मुझे ।

उम्मीद ही थी अंतिम सहारा लेकिन उम्मीद भी रह गई अधूरी

Atul Kumar

He is Atul Kumar .He never underestimate any person .He is amiable to all.He takes his wake up call.

(1)

इश्क़ में बहुत से रिस्क है ।
पर मज़ा आता करने में इश्क़ है ।
इश्क़ होता केवल एक बार है ।
इसके बिना ज़िन्दगी लगती बेकार है ।

इश्क़ ज़ाहिर करने के बहुत से तरीके है ।
इश्क़ के बिना ज़िन्दगी रुकी सी है ।
इश्क़ बिना रूह को मिलता नही सुकून है ।
इश्क़ का पहला पड़ाव यकीन है ।
इश्क़ से ही तो ज़िन्दगी हसीन है।

Samikhya Swain (Ikhya)

Ikhya hails from silver city Cuttack. Currently she is a student of class 12. She loves to write because she believes that words can create wonders. You can connect with her using her Instagram ID @triggered.ladki or simply drop a mail at samikhya123swain@gmail.com

(1)

Dear Love

Deep inside the melancholy heart,
There stood some broken memories.
Passing through the waves of life,
Struggling in the ups and downs with the streams.

It seems,
I was achingly loving my life,
Where the hate still brews somewhere beneath.

Oh! It's just enough of heightens,
That stopped my heart mangle
And made it yours by any wangle.

Dearie,
I wanna be like how you loved me!

Dulgach Pooja Singh

Loves watching cricket
Reading novels
 writing stories
Teaching and nature lover

(1)

Uska mera ghar ka pass aana aur apne dosto k sath cricket khelna, vo bahan dhundhne ki muja bahar bulana bina baat meri khidki ka kaanch dhoot na meri dadi ka pass gali sun kr b muja muskura kr dekhna

Ice cream wala aata he mera ghar na aangan ma theen char ice cream milna

Mera chup chup kr usa khidki se dekhna

Kabhi chit pr jaa kr dekhna too

Kabhi kitchen ki khidki se thaak na

Kabhi muja dukan pr bulna aur mooft ka saman dana

Teej tyohar pr muja apne chota bhai bhen se toofa bajna

ghar se bahar jata he uska dost muja bhabhi bhabhi bolna

Mela me muja chup k se milna aur mithai dena

Mera janamdin ka pura mohala M bhandar karva na

Ko se gaya he ab ye he mohalla wala ishq

Ab in badi badi imarato ma

Ab too sirf what app pr he baatha hoti h aur vahi pr he breakup hota h Na koi dost bhabhi bolta h

Na icecream milti h

Ab to bs bade bade mool ma milta h aur na kisi se daarta h

Na kisi izzat ki pavar karta h aur haato ma haat laka firrta h

Muskan Sachdeva

Muskan Sachdeva hails from Basti, uttar Pradesh. She completed studies from St. Basil's and is pursuing Chartered accountant along with bcom from Allahabad university. Writing was just a time pass earlier but then it became her passion. She has been co-authored in 10+ anthologies.

Love Of Life

Love sometimes hurts but moving on is the best medicine. May be god broke you to give you someone who you deserve more. No one knows whom she/he deserves.

Breakup happens but moving on is what I think more helpful. Being sad and crying for someone is a fullish act as the one who left will never come back.

I had breakups I cried for the person but then I thought moving on and loving someone who actually loves me and wants me is better. I m happy even after I moved on with new person.

Being happy is what everyone wants. If crying brings someone back then only crying is remedy but crying never brings someone back. Crying n praising a person to come back in life makes that person take you for granted and also you loose your self respect and self esteem in front of them.

Moving on is also not easy. If there are some medicine for moving on then every person would have taken it. It's not easy to forget moments and time spent with your loved ones but at the end there is no remedy. Forgetting moments and thinking of family and yourself is what make things little better.

I moved on with a person who loves me cares for me wants me in his life respects me and for whom I m everything. He loves me to no extent. Being with him and talking to him makes me happy. I live for him. I m me with him. And I just love him the most.

Prachi Gupta

Prachi Gupta is a student of BBA, hai ling from Allahabad, UP. She is fond of watching movies, travelling and cooking. Although, she loves writing and singing as, she believes scribble your thoughts on a blank paper can remove your stress and makes a person happy. Along with this, she is a Digital Marketer and a writer who has been a co-author of many anthologies.

Follow her on instagram:- @_prachi_gupta_210

About You

Love endured me from inside
Love gives me a little hard sight.

When, I firstly saw you in my balcony
I just became your lover in just a slight eyesight.

When I think you,
I lose my consciousness in a bright light.

Your love inspires me in a dark night.
Your love drives me in another side.

After your forthcoming,
I start "Dreaming About You And Me"..

Saurabh Rajput

He is saurabh rajput.He is not a writer really as per him he just let his feelings express into words..   he is student of 12th..he love listing music..

Moholle Wala Ishq..

Jinhe ek Pal dekhne ko
Ghanto tak khud ko sawara karta tha..
Khi aaj v jwa hai mujhme
Wahi moholle wala ishq..
Unka mujhe ek tak dekhna..
Aur Mera ghanto tak bate Karna..
Har najar me jwa tajgi Ka milna..
Aisa tha moholle wala ishq..
Na rasto ki prwaah..
Na Auro ka gum tha..
Bepanah thi mohhbat..
Na sitam gar sitam tha..
Bs unki muskurahat thi..yhi tha khuda Ka Karan..
Meri to aarju wahi..wahi thi mehram
Lage aaj v jwa hai mujhme..
Wo moholle wala ishq..

Pragya Kapil

Her name is Pragya kapil and she is pursuing her graduation from Banasthali University ,Jaipur. She is a student and a writer both....she writes whatever she feels...just pen down her emotions which turns out to be a poem

मोहल्ले वाला प्यार –

आज चलते चलते किसी से कुछ ऐसी नज़रे लड़ी की नज़रे झुकाने का मन
ही ना किया,

ऐसे डूबी मानो जैसे कोई गोताखोर समंदर की गहराइयों में डूबता हो,

बस देखते ही देखते हमे उनकी मौजूदगी जचने लगी,

कभी वो हम मे खोए कभी हम उनमें,

धीरे धीरे करीब आते गए,

नजदीकियां बढ़ी,

प्यार का मतलब समझ आए इतना तो नहीं था,

पर जो भी था दिल में एक अजीब सी लहर दौड़ पड़ती थी,

ना जाने उसके ना दिखने पर बेचैनी सी क्यू होती थी,

ना जाने मन मानने को तैयार ना था,

सब कुछ जानते हुए भी अंजना सा बन कर अडा था,

जैसा भी हो जो भी हो,

आखिर वो मेरा मोहल्ले वाला प्यार था,

कुछ ना बोले, कुछ ना तोले,

बस सिर्फ देखने का ही मोहताज था,

बस ऐसा ही मेरा मोहल्ले वाला प्यार था।

आंखों की गुस्ताखियां –

उनका पलके झुकना और फिर मुस्कुराना,
हा हमे अच्छा लगता था
उनका यू देर रात तक हमे देखने के लिए
उनकी छत पर मंडराना,
हा हमे अच्छा लगता था
उनका यूं टेढ़ी नज़रों से हमे रोज़ छेड कर जाना,
हा हमे अच्छा लगता था
बस चाहते तो हम ये ही थे
की बिन कुछ कहे बिना कुछ सुने
हम उन्हें और वो हमे यूं ही देखते रहे
वो अपनी छत पर और हम अपनी छत पर
यूं ही एक प्यारी सी मुस्कान लिए,
एक दूसरे को छेडते रहे।

Aarti Mahala

Aarti mahala pursing Bsc hons.   in agriculture from Sriganganagar.

She is from Sikar.

Writing means happiness to her. Write until your hobby become your passion.

She loves to spread happiness to people .

Love

Love takes you high ,
Away from all WiFi.
Dancing in dreams ,
Life is full of creams.
Love bring sunshine,
Like party full of wine.
Laughing at yawns,
Missing in every dawn.
A love is so precious ,
A love so true,
A love that comes from me to you...

To Mah Love

You're special to me.
You're the only one who i wouldn't mind loosing sleep for, the only one who i can never get tired of talking to and the only one who crosses my mind constantly throughout the day.

You're the only one who can make me smile without trying, bring down my mood without the intention and affect my emotions with every action of yours. I can't explain with just words how much you mean to me but you're the one I'm afraid of losing and the one I want to keep in my life.

प्यार सूकून है

पास होना जरूरी नहीं,
बस साथ की बात है...
जैसे ढलती तो हर रात है,
लेकिन राहत तो तुम्हारे साथ हैं...
क्योंकि तू जरूरत नहीं , सुकून है मेरा।
इश्क़ में बदलते देखा है,
 लेकिन तुमने तो सुधारा है...
तुम यक़ीन ना भी करो,
लेकिन तुम्हारी दुआ ने नेक इंसान बनाया है...
क्योंकि तू जरूरत नहीं, सुकून है मेरा।

Anmol Chugh Dildard

Anmol Chugh Dildard is a student of civil engineering at St. Soldier group of institutions. He is from Jalandhar City, Punjab. He is love to read and write thoughts and poetry. He is belong from middle class family. He has participated in many anthologies.

"प्यार के गीत"

प्यार के गीत गाते रहो,
ज़िन्दगी में तुम सदा मुस्कुराते रहो,
गम को सदा दबाते रहो,
बस दुनिया को खुशी जताते रहो,
गम हो चाहे ना हो,
हर पल खुशी के गीत गाते रहो..!!

"प्यार"

देखने में तो बहुत आसान है,
साहिब;
ये प्यार है,
कोई खेल का मैदान नहीं है,
देखने में तो आसान है,
पर प्यार एक इम्तिहान है..!!

"पल भर का प्यार"

पल भर का प्यार था,
बड़ा ही बेशुमार था,
खींच लाया मुझे तेरी ओर,
ये कैसा तेरा विश्वास था..!!

Siya Golani

Siya golani is a creative writer. She has inclination to positive aspects of life. She is a confident presenter who keeps her views very subtle but firmly. She evokes her messages and effectively engages the audience through her writeups.

Love

Love seems such a small word, a four letter word but when this word enters the life it shines the surroundings and gives a strong adrenalin rush. Love is a drug which makes our life worth living. It is said that everything is fair in love and war, well said but nowadays this four letter word LOVE is very rare. Strong love for someone makes you feel responsible about the situation and the one properly fulfils that responsibility comes first in the race of finding true love. Always remember Love is easy to find but its very difficult to be dedicated and loyal. Give your best because this can change your life forever. Everyone likes to fall in love at first sight but please believe in second look.

इश्क

इश्क तो कमबख्तथा पर दिल पर थोड़ा सख्त था।
भूलके सारे काम बस याद आता है अब एक ही नाम, हाँ एक ही
नाम, दिन, रात और शाम।

कुछ लोगों ने कहा यह पागलपन है।
और कुछ ने कहा ये ही सबसे बड़ा संगम है।

थामकर उसका हाथ निकल पड़ा हूँ उसके साथ।
काफी कोशिश की है कहने की, पर किस्मत ने भी ठानी है साथ न
देने की।

पर भी यह कोशिश जारी है और मन को ये ही समझाया है की अब
अपनी बारी है।

Ujjwal Shree

Ujjwal shree with her pen name Neha Gupta is from Patna, Bihar

She is an avid writer, poetess, and artist. She loves to play with words and write from the depth of her heart. She always express her emotions through words rather than saying. She generally writes about Motivation, emotions, pain and abstract. Writing helps her to survive in her worst phase of life. Writing is just like breathing to her because when she feels depressed she used to write her feelings.

Follow her on Instagram : @Shree22349

Email Id : ng223494@gmail.com

The Secret Lover

I was sitting by the window

Looking at life , thinking that maybe I've become a spectator to my own life fading away like a beautiful tree being reduced to a trunkless object

I didn't realise that someone was impatiently waiting by the window trying to get my attention

A boy probably of my own age with a hand full of beautiful mesmerising red roses

I couldn't wait myself so I motioned him to wait and was about to take out my purse

But something stopped me , deep down I knew it wasn't something but 'someone' who showed me that love as a thought is far more beautiful than the reality

I simply gave up everything surrounding him so I didn't want to remind myself of all endless roses he gave me still lying somewhere Among my most priceless possessions

I again faced the young boy and opened my window and excused myself by saying

"Aaj change nahi hai , sorry" (I don't have change today)

He didn't say anything just looked at me and then at the
traffic light which now signalled GREEN

"Ye aapke liye" (this is for you) hé handed me one of the
most beautiful rose from his bouquet

Maybe you don't always have to be in love to feel love ?

Reality of Perfection

Will you marry me?" he somehow managed to bend down on
knees.

The delightful red rose in her grey hair,
simply said "Yes" one more time!

Amita Prabhakar

Amita Prabhakar, is a young and dynamic lady in her early 30's. She belongs to the 'Jhoomka' city of Bareilly. She has just completed her B.Ed exams from MJPRU. A bubbly girl who loves to write, who writes to express, her written expressions always impress. She is determined to bring the best out of her.She loves traveling like hell, she has the quantum of everlasting quest when it comes to explore places. She loves to spend the life not for merely 'chalta hai' attitude rather she takes her life as an opportunity to know the world and make the world see through her tiny window which she has created.She is a lovely mother of two childrens. They are still in their first stages of life spending most of the time exploring between their school bag and lunch box. She is very fond of teaching kids, her array in teaching is magnanimous. She believes that the life is a journey till pyre and we are mare passingers.

तुम्हारा दिल ख़ज़ाना हैं

तुमसे मेरा रिश्ता पुराना है;

तुमसे मिलना तो एक बहाना हैं;

हकीक़त में तो तुम्हें पाना है;

क्योंकि तेरा दिल, दिल नहीं एक ख़ज़ाना है;

तेरा प्यार पाना है तुझे अपना बनाना है;

सपनों में तेरे आना है तेरी नींदे चुराना हैं;

क्योंकि तेरा दिल, दिल नहीं ख़ज़ाना हैं;

तेरे साथ यादें बनाना है तू ही जीने का बहाना हैं;

तुझको खोके कुछ नहीं पाना है;

अपनी मीठी मीठी बातों में तुझको फसाना है;

क्योंकि तेरा दिल, दिल नहीं एक ख़ज़ाना हैं;

घर पे बहाने बनना हैं तुझसे मिलने आना हैं;

तेरी आँखों की गहराईयों में खोके तेरे दिल में उतर जाना हैं;

तू ही हसरत तू ही जीने का बहाना हैं;

तुझे ही हर हाल में पाना हैं;

माँ - बाप को तू ही पसंद आना हैं;

क्योंकि तेरा दिल, दिल नहीं एक ख़ज़ाना हैं;

तुझसे रिश्ता बना के जिंदगी भर साथ निभाना हैं;

तेरे नाम की मेहंदी लगाना है, तेरे नाम का सिंदूर लगाना है;

तेरे साथ ही घर बसाना है;

तेरी बीवी बन जाना हैं;

क्योंकि तेरा दिल, दिल नहीं एक ख़ज़ाना हैं....

Lokesh Upadhyay.

Lokesh Upadhyay, resident of buxar district in Bihar, presently he is a student in class 12th Dandi Swami sahajanand saint Vinova college. He has a keen interest in writing his heart out in the form of small poems, porses and verses. He hope you will enjoy reading his work and appreciate it.

Thank you..

मुहल्ले वाला प्यार

अच्छा अजीब होता है न मुहल्ले वाला हमारा प्यार भी

मतलब दूर दूर तक कोई रिश्ता-नाता नहीं रहता,

फिर अचानक से वो आती है मेरे मुहल्ले में ,

और देखते देखते ही एक अजीब सी चाहत होती है दिल में कि काश

उससे बात हो जाए,

ज्यादा कुछ नहीं फिर भी दोस्ती हो जाए,

लेकिन वो तो नकचढी है ये कहाँ हमें मालूम होता है,

जोरन लेने के बहाने जाता हूं,

उसके घर का दरवाजा खटखटाता हूं,

लेकिन अंदर से कुछ आवाज न आने की वजह से थोड़ा गुस्से से एक

बार और खटखटाता हूं तो अंदर से आवाज़, आती है ,

किसका दिमाग खराब है आराम से, तोड़ दोगे क्या?

उसके बाद मेरी हालत खराब___

फिर भी हिम्मत करते हुए मैं दरवाजे के सामने बेचारा बन के खड़ा

था,

और उधर वो मुझे देखते ही अंदर चली गई और एक गुस्से में आवाज़

सुनाई दी ,

कि मम्मी जाओ देखो कोई मुहल्ले का लफंगा आया है,

अब ये सुनते ही मेरे चेहरे का रंग फीका पड़ जाता है,

फिर भी हिम्मत न हारी और डटा रहा ,

उसकी मम्मी आई बोली क्या है बेटा?

फिर मेरा वहीं बहाना ,

डरते_डरते आंटी जोरन मिलेगा क्या?

फिर वो बोलती है ,

रूबी भईया को थोड़ा सा जोरन लाकर दे दो,

अब सही बोला जाए तो दिल बस इतना ही कर रहा था कि चल दें
लेकिन हिम्मत ना हारा और रुका रहा,
[लेकीन एक बात की खुशी थी कि उनका नाम पता तो चला,]
एक बार फिर उनकी गुस्से वाली आवाज़,,
मम्मी मैंने बोला है ना किसी के साथ मेरा रिश्ता ना बनाओ,
मैं इसको भईया नहीं बोलने वाली,
जो भी हो ये बात सुन के दिल को सुकून मिला,
वहाँ से शुरु हुई ,
उसके बाद होती रही,
शाम को छत पे,
एसे रास्ते में आते_जाते
फिर धीरे धीरे मै भी उनको पसंद आया और आखिर वो मेरी हो ही
गई।

जोरन(दही बनाने के लिए दूध में थोड़ा सा दही डाला जाता है
उसको ही जोरन बोलते है)

Ashwini Kumar Singh

He is Ashwini Kumar Singh , a student of B. Pharmacy . He has been writing quotes and short poems since a long time back , but never thought of writing them for publication purpose . Its due to his friend that he has entered in this field .

Truly divine feeling : Love

Love ;
What is it ?
Merely attraction between two hearts?
No , it's between souls .
Lord Sun gives us light ;
By which we survive ,
This is also his love for us .
Rivers gives us water ,
Which is needed for survival ,
This is also a selfless love .
Deeply rooted tree ,
Gives fruits for free ,
Provides shelter to birds ,
Isn't this is pure love ?
Who says ; " love is blind "
Rather it's purely divine .
True love never binds ,
It sets us free ,
Just like wide spread branches of tree...

Richa Gurudas Mayenkar

Richa is a Student , who loves to write poetry. she is passionate writer and always love to be in writing mood. she is persuing her B.Ed degree and has habbit of Blog writing.

Yeh Safar Pyaar Ka

Ek aarzu hai humari zara sunle,
Pyaar ki baat hai , dil aur dadkan ko kahiye.

Aaj hai voh din aya,
Aaj voh waqt hai tham gaya.
Aaj ishq parwan chadha hai,
Dil ka izhaar dil se hua hai.

voh chupte - chupte aapko dekhna,
Aapke samne aane se saansein rukh jana,
Door hokar bhi aapke pass hona,
Har pal aapke bare main sochna.

Aaj khatam hone waala hai yeh safar,
Kuch khatti-mitthi yaadon ke saath
Aaj shuru hone wala hai naya safar,
Humara aapke saath.

Yeh safar hai chahato ka ,
Yeh safar hai pyaar ka.

Parul Sunder

loves to write and have good speaking skills as well

जीने का आसरा

दोनों ने किया था प्यार ,इजहार, इकरार,

पर तुम क्यों भूल गए ।

आज वो बदल गए,

कल तक हमारे दिल में रहते थे।

मैं वही हूँ तुम कहीं दूर चल गए,

क्यों कसमे वादे तोड़ गए।

क्यों बीती बाते भूल गए,

क्या खता थी हमारी।

जो हमें जीते जी छोड़ गए,

पहले जिंदगी छीनी मुझसे मेरी,

अब मौत भी छीन ली,

साथ- साथ चलने का फैसला भी तेरा था,

रास्ता बदलने का फैसला भी तेरा है,

अब तू आए या ना आए।

मुझे कुछ फर्क नहीं पड़ता

क्यूंकि दर्द ही अब मेरा प्यार है ।

इस दर्द को अपना यार और प्यार बना लिया,

अपने जीने का आसरा बना लिया।

प्यार

ना चाहते हुए भी तुझसे प्यार हो गया,

तेरे रंग- रूप, हुस्न का दीवाना हो गया,

खुली जुल्फे, झुकी नजरों का मैं कायल हो गया,

हर धड़कन में चाहत तेरी,

सांसों में खुशबू तेरी,

हर वक्त तुझे याद करने को जी करता है।

कैसे समझाऊं इस दिल को,

हर तमन्ना हर एहसास है तू मेरा।

कैसे एहसास दिलाओ,

मैं अरसे से खामोश हूं,

वह अरसे से बेखबर,

दिल में तू जुबा पर तेरी बातें रहती है

भूल जाएगा जिस दिन यह दिल तुम्हें

शायद वो जिंदगी का आखरी दिन होगा

Lakshman Mulchandani

He is Laksh. He is not a writer really as per him he just let his feelings turn into words and wonder what it conveys to you. For him writing on his diary (named as Aashi) is the best way to express his emotions. He is going to join his first year in NIT Raipur. A perfect balance between Shinchan and Kazama. He is a big admirer of Naruto (series) and indian epics. Music is his heartbeat.

मासूमियत का साथ

मन की बात है,
दिल ने कही है,
वो पास नहीं पर दूर भी नहीं है।
और तो दिल की बात करते है,
लेकिन मेरे हर सैल में बसी है।

बचपन की दोस्त है,
मासूमियत का साथ है,
उसमें मेरी और मुझमें उसकी छाप है,
लिखा मैंने आज है पर फिर भी वो यह मुझसे पहले से जानती है।
मुझसे ज्यादा वो मुझे पहचानती है।

बर्थ- दे था आज उसका,
दिल से थी दुआ,
जिए वह हज़ारों साल,
साल में खुशियां मिले हज़ार,
हैपी बर्थडे यार,
मिसिंग यू सो मच आशि।

Hoping You

Every Night,
When i close my eyes,
Its your face that comes in my sight,
Then ....i just want to get lost in those dreamy lies.

Its been so long,
Still wondering,why was it all so wrong?
Wondering was it for my loss or for my gain?
As there was so much pleasure followed by pain.

At times it feels that sepration was needed,
To clarify was it true or just our hormones cheated,
Then sometimes i just i can't bear it anymore,
I just want to meet you atleast once more.

Recently i have started believing in power of want,
And that magic which connected us,
I'll just do everything so that my wish get grant,
I m waiting for that unexpected meeting maybe in a
gurudwara or a bus.

Do you also still feel that spark?,
Willing to reignite that fire,
As,no matter how much dark,
You are the moonlight that i'll always admire.

Riya Srivastava

Poet by passion and entrepreneur by action.Her words feel the real emotions and love and connect with the heart of peoples.Follow her on instagram @riyashrivastava2000

Tera Intezaar...

In ankho ko tera intezaar aj bhi h,
Tere hone ka ehsaas tere bad bhi h,
Tu wo saya h meri zindgi ka ,
Tujhse hi mere din aur meri raat bhi h...

Tujhse hi din ka ujala aur shaam bhi h,
Tujhse hi mere zindagi ka saar bhi h,
Tu h to dhadkan bhi khil jati h,
Tujhse hi mere din aur meri raat bhi h....

Dil Ki Tamanna......

Bs ek aarzoo dil me har baar aati h,
Tere sath zindagi bite yhi ardaas aati h,
Tere na hone se zindgi sochi hi ni maine,
Tu dur hoke bhi mere paas hoti h.......

Dil ki tamannao me is kadar tera saya h,
Laakh bhulna chahu tb bhi tujhe apne aas pas paya h,
Tu mere dil ki wo khwahish h,
Jo hr din har pal mujhe ek achha insaan bnaya h..........

Ayesha Rajpal

Ayesha Rajpal is writer by passion. She is into nobel profession of teaching and runs an academy in Delhi. She is fun lovung and easy going person and has been co author for few books . She is into writing poems . Even she loves calligraphy and Mandala art too.

My Sunshine

You are sunshine to my life
It is hard to believe that you are mine
My eyes will tell you
How much I love you

My Love for you is so deep
When you became mine I was on cloud nine
You are king of my heart
And will never let you be apart
You are sunshine to my life
It is hard to believe that you are mine

No matter what may come and what may go
You'll stay with me forever
Hold my hand and take me to your world
It's only you who can make feel young
You are sunshine to my life
It is hard to believe that you are mine

Shobha Rajpal

Shobha Rajpal is writer by passion. Her love for hindi is divine. She feels quite comfortable with hindi rather english as she loves her mother tongue. She is Hindi graduated and teacher by profession.

मोहल्ला वाला इश्क

इधर कोरोना और लॉक डाउन
ने सताया
घर मे बन्द लोगो को रुलाया
किसी को कुछ भी समझ न आया
हर शख्स अपने हाल से घबराया
हमारे मोहल्ले में एक प्रेमी युगल नजर आया
जिसने इस लॉक डाउन का फायदा उठाया
आंखों ही आंखों में करते थे बाते
रातो में छतों पर होती थी मुलाकाते
उनका दिल लेने देने का मौसम आया था
फूलो पर बहारो का मौसम छाया था
इन दोनों ने लॉक डाउन के सभी दर्दो को भुलाया था
और यही लव मोहल्ला वाला इश्क कहलाया था

Vedika Agarwal

She is Vedika Agarwal a student of Bsc home science, Delhi university. She likes to write and draw a sketch. She is passionate for dancing, singing and acting. She is a determined, bold and a kind hearted girl. She is very conducive in nature. She loves to spend her leisure with old age home people and orphanage children. She loves to learn new things. She is a very emotional girl. She loves to help others.

Daastan E Mohalla Ishq

Voh bhi kya dinn the
Jab hum kisi ke intezaar ke liye taraste the
Aur us intezar mei jo etbar tha pyar ka

Uska voh hume dekhke muskurana Aur humare dil ka khwabo
mein doob jana
Uska voh humare ruthne pe mnana Aur humare ansu se aitraz
karna

Voh bhi kya dinn the
Humko daatke smjhana aur hmare Udasi mei udas hona
Apni Choti Choti Pagal pantiyo se humko hasana

jab Hum apni chat pe unke deedar kar intezar krte the
Ki ek jhalak ek nazar ek ehsas ho jaye
Par unhe kya maloom tha ki koi hmari ek jhalak dekhne ke liye
Pagal tha

Voh jo unke Ek Ada pe hmari ankhein jhukana
Yun Pagal sa ban jana
Jaise Koi leher Hmare dil ko chukar guzar gyi ho

Voh bhi kya dinn the
Voh jo unko takleef m dekhke
Hmare dil m dard hona

Uska uss mohalla ke bahar se nikalna
Aur fir uski Khushboo ka mehekna yun hasi si la deta tha

Ab sawarna chhod diya h humne
Kyunki jisse hum Sada psand h toh sawarna ki zaroorat nai
Usse hmari khoobsoorti se pyr nai tha
Usse pyr tha toh hmare dil se tha, hmari muskan Se tha Aur
hmari har ek Ada se

Voh jab jab Hmara haath thamke chla krte thay
Aisa Lagta tha jaise puri Duniya hume mil gyi ho

Par kya Kare aaj ek aise Daur m aake khade hogye h
Jaha unhe Bta bhi nai sakte ki yeh dil unke liye aaj bhi
dhadakta hai
Aur yeh Pyar aaj bhi Unka liye utna hi hai

Flairs and Glairs, a platform by a student for the students. We are esteemed youth struggling to carve out our path for our future and we follow a basic mindset Since everyone is not born with all-round skills. Joining hands with people who are born to execute it with perfection is the best way to evolve. Self-Evolution is the need of the hour but, evolving as a community is what we strive for. The initiative as kickstarted by, Founder- Mr. Shubham Shah with the motive to utilize the skillset and talent of writing has now a team of 10+ people who are actively participating into newer forms of learning and discovering talents among youngsters. We Provide platform and services like Publishing opportunities, Open mics, Workshops, Hands-on training. Operating with Brand Name Of Flairs and Glairs (Publication House), we offer the chance of elevating a passionate writer to an esteemed author With Brand name Teekhe Zasbaaat, We bring to you an opportunity to get accustomed with the Public Speaking and Presenting of Thoughts along with regular challenges to brush up your inking spirit. The newest initiative to extend our services we introduced in a new writing Platform- The Glittering Fables and Ink Over Tears.

We Choose to Fly Like A Falcon than to be a

Leg Pulling Crab.

To Know More: Infoline – 7781900870

Mail Us At-

flairsandglairs@gmail.com / info@flairsandglairs.in

Or Visit is at

www.flairsandglairs.com / www.flairsandglairs.in

Social Handles- @flairsandglairs @teekhezasbaaat